CW00968377

Hi! I'm Katie and I am 8 years old. Max is my older brother. He's really clever. He helps me with my home work when I'm stuck. He knows everything! But don't tell him I said that. He can get really annoying and know-it-all. He is always telling me stuff, but sometimes it's just too much. All I want is a simple answer, like 'yes' or 'no'. Instead, it's always 'maybe, because...' So annoying.

But he's not so bad. He always looks out for me. And we have fun playing games together.

I think my favourite thing is playing outside in any weather! I love going to the park, especially the adventure playground with the huge, curly slide. You can go really fast on that one, especially when you lie down! Mum hates it when I come home covered in mud, but I can't help it. The fun parts of the park are always the muddiest.

Hey, I'm Max and I'm 11. I love reading. I read comics and cartoons that make me laugh, and I read adventure stories about knights and castles, or pirates and buried treasure! Mum is always telling me I have an over-active imagination. I can't help it. My mind just starts picturing loads of weird stuff.

I also love solving puzzles. Grandpa always buys me books full of word-searches and crosswords. I like to time myself and see how fast I can solve them.

Katie is my younger sister. She is really energetic and fun to be around. She's really fast and sporty. I wish I could be as good as her at sports. But don't tell her I said that. She can also be really annoying, when she can't sit still for more than five minutes. And she doesn't stop talking!

But she's cool. I'm pleased she's my sister.

1

"This is soooo boring," moaned Katie, throwing down her pencil.

Max and Katie were sitting at the kitchen table doing their homework. They had only started ten minutes ago, but Katie was already complaining.

"You've only just started!" laughed Max.

"Exactly!" agreed Mum. "The sooner you start, the sooner you'll finish!"

Katie's shoulders slumped forward even more. She was resting her chin on her up-turned palm. She knew they were right. It just wasn't that easy. She had to write the opening of a story but she didn't know where to start.

"Mrs Allen is so strict," complained Katie. "I wish I didn't have to go to school."

Katie's imagination started wandering. She was thinking up some elaborate excuses for her

homework not being finished. Perhaps next door's dog escaped and chewed her book to shreds; perhaps she accidentally dropped her work in the mud on the way to school; perhaps an angry seagull attacked her and she had to use her book as a shield, which the seagull pecked and pecked at until all the tiny pieces of paper had blown away in a single gust of wind.

Before Katie could decide on the most believable excuse, the doorbell rang. Katie sat up straight, Max's pencil stopped writing and hovered above his page, waiting. They listened to Mum at the door and they knew the signs. They knew it was the postman. They knew it was time for another adventure.

This was much better than homework.

Before Mum could argue, they snapped their books shut, lifted the time machine from Mum's arms and scrambled up the stairs.

Safely behind the closed door of Max's bedroom, they found the Mission Plan.

Mission Plan

Place: Victorian England
Date: AD 1871

A wealthy couple called Mr and Mrs Green find out that they have been robbed. Someone has taken the lady's finest jewellery from her locked bedroom. The only other person to have a key to the room is the servant girl, Peggy.

Peggy is innocent, but Mr and Mrs Green don't believe her. Who else could it be? Peggy loses her job. She struggles to find another job and cannot support her family. She finds herself homeless, unhappy and with no hope.

Task:

Can you help Peggy keep her job by finding the real thief?

2

"I learnt about the Victorians at school this year!" exclaimed Katie. "Queen Victoria was on the throne for ages and the ladies wore pretty dresses and... and... and they built grand houses and liked going to the seaside!"

"And our school play was 'Oliver Twist' by Charles Dickens last year!" replied Max. "Remember? It was about an orphan who escaped to the city, where he became a pick-pocket."

Katie suddenly looked less excited about visiting the Victorian era. "I remember we all played lots of poor children with nowhere to live," she said. "Everyone wore ripped costumes and had dirty faces."

This side of the Victorians was less pleasant.

"We must still have our costumes somewhere," said Katie, jumping up.

"Great idea!" replied Max.

They pulled a battered cardboard box out from beneath Max's bed and found their Victorian costumes inside.

Katie wore a dark green dress with laced-up boots. She pulled a white apron over the top, then tied ribbons in her hair.

Max wore short trousers with black shoes. He put on a white shirt with a waistcoat, followed by a dark green flat cap.

They looked the part now.

3

They read the history booklet and were both amazed by how much happened during Victoria's reign.

"The Victorians invented so many cool things that we still use today," said Max. "It was a time of real change."

Katie was pointing at the picture of a Penny Farthing.

"Look at their bikes!" she laughed. "They look so silly!"

Max agreed. "It seems strange that they couldn't work out how to make a bike with a chain, but they could dig massive tunnels and make a train travel safely deep underground!"

They read about Queen Victoria and how she only wore black for decades after her husband died. They read about the changes in transport, from steam engines to the first petrol cars. They read about the terrible conditions for many people who lived in the slums in the cities, compared with the men who got richer from building factories.

Max found the Time Travel Sticker and passed it to Katie. It showed Queen Victoria's face, like a stamp.

"This looks like the Penny Black," explained Max. "This was the world's first proper stamp for posting letters!"

They looked in the mirror. They were ready for their adventure.

The Time Machine was especially slow to start this time.

"What if the Time Machine stops working while we're somewhere in history on an adventure?" asked Kate with worried eyes.

"It will always have enough power to bring us home," he said confidently.

Katie was happy. Her big brother knew everything. She hoped she would be as clever as him when she was eleven.

Max felt uncomfortable. He didn't like lying to his sister. But he had just made that up to make her feel better. He was also worried they might not make it home.

Max programmed the Time Machine and they got ready for the journey.

Colours and sparks started to spin around them and the room started to merge together until they felt themselves travelling through time.

4

Max and Katie felt the ground become solid again beneath their feet and looked around. They were standing on a busy street that was paved with cobbled stones. Horses' hooves clip-clopped as they pulled covered carriages on rickety wheels.

Ladies with long skirts and bonnets were admiring the displays in shop windows and gentlemen with tall hats and long coats leaned on canes while talking in groups, sometimes stroking their long moustaches.

Max looked at the buildings. They were tall houses, four stories high, with grand steps leading up to a covered entrance. The front doors were painted in bold colours: bright red, navy blue, jet black. Brass knockers and handles gleamed in the autumn sun.

Katie was busy admiring the beautiful dress of a lady nearby, when they heard someone sobbing.

At the top of a set of nearby steps was a well-dressed couple who looked very angry and upset. A girl dressed as a servant was crying and begging them, but the gentleman was pointing away. They wanted her to leave.

Max and Katie saw the couple disappear inside the house and heard the door slam shut.

"That must be Peggy," whispered Max. "Let's go and talk to her."

They approached the sobbing lady, who was now sitting on the bottom step. Katie held out a handkerchief.

"Thank you," she said as she sniffed into the handkerchief.

"You're welcome. I'm Katie and this is Max, my big brother," replied Katie.

"I'm Peggy. Oh, what a terrible morning! It's not my fault, it really isn't."

Katie sat down beside her on the step. "What's happened? Maybe we can help."

"This was my first week at work," she explained. "I really like it here too. But something valuable has gone missing. They think... they think... they think I took it!" she wailed. "Just because my father is in prison for stealing, doesn't mean I took it! And he only took some bread because we were hungry. I know that doesn't make it right, but the little ones wouldn't stop crying with hunger."

Her shoulders shook as she sobbed uncontrollably.

Max waited until she had calmed down before he spoke. It took a while.

"What was taken and where was it taken from?" he asked gently.

"It was Mistress Green's jewellery, her favourite necklace with matching bracelet. Really beautiful pieces," replied Peggy.

"Where was it taken from?" asked Katie.

She blew her nose noisily into the handkerchief before replying.

"The Master and Mistress's bedroom, of course," replied Peggy. "She keeps everything there inside a wooden jewellery box. It has a little ballerina that dances when you turn the handle. It's really lovely."

"Don't worry, we're going to help you," he said.

"The only way is to find out who the real thief is."

Katie nodded. "Yes, you need to start by telling us everything that happened today."

Peggy wiped her nose and looked into the distance. "Well, it was a normal morning," she started. "Me and the other servant, Eliza, went about our duties as normal. There were some deliveries, but they only came to the servants' entrance. The only people who came inside the house were the chimney sweeps, but they were watched the whole time. Nobody else that I know of came into the house."

Max and Katie looked at each other.

"How do you know the chimney sweeps were watched the whole time?" asked Max.

"Because it was me who watched them! I was with them the whole time," she explained. "I thought there was something very suspicious about the man, so I stayed with them in every room they went into. All morning. I know they can't have taken anything because they never went into that room."

"What about Eliza?" asked Max. "Could she have taken it?"

Peggy shook her head. "She was helping the Mistress with her new dress and hat which were delivered earlier and they were together the whole time in the drawing room. Besides, the room was locked and I am the only person who had a key. It's just impossible. I'm the only suspect."

5

Max and Katie were quiet for a moment, thinking.

"Eliza was busy and has an alibi," said Max. "So it must be the chimney sweep."

"Yes!" agreed Katie. "And you said he looked suspicious. There must be some way that he deceived you. Perhaps he slipped out without you knowing while you were distracted?"

"But that's impossible!" shrieked Peggy. "I locked us into the room and followed them downstairs afterwards. Besides, the bedroom door where the jewellery was stolen from was also locked. There is no way that he could have stolen anything."

Max didn't know where to start.

"How can we find this chimney sweep?" he asked.

"I don't know. They probably live over in the slums. No, wait, that's them!" said Peggy, pointing across the street.

Max followed her gaze across the street, where a man in tatty clothes and a boy covered in soot were walking. They carried large brushes.

Max thought this was as good a place to start as any. Max and Katie arranged to meet Peggy at Mr and Mrs Green's house at six o'clock, then set off after the chimney sweeps.

They soon reached a street corner, where the man pushed the door of a public house open and

disappeared inside the smoke-filled room. The boy continued walking down the street.

"Shall we split up?" asked Katie.

"No," replied Max. "That man looks dangerous. I think we should make friends with that boy, see if we can get him to talk instead. He must have seen something."

Katie was relieved at this answer. She agreed. She didn't like the idea of one of them being caught by that angry man.

They followed the boy from a distance and watched him take a coin from his pocket. He bought a bread roll from a lady with a basket full of bread, then walked on to a corner.

"What's he doing?" asked Katie. "Why isn't he eating that roll? He's really skinny, he must be starving!"

They didn't have to wait long before Katie's question was answered.

6

The boy was waiting outside a school building. The playground was empty when he arrived, but soon the bell in the little tower on top of the school started ringing.

Children started leaving the school doors. It was lunch time. Groups of girls played hopscotch, while boys found pebbles to aim at a larger stone that was the target.

Soon, a girl with a white apron and ribbons in her hair came to the gate to meet the boy, who gave her the bread roll.

Max and Katie watched as the two children chatted.

"He's brought her lunch," said Katie. "Maybe they're brother and sister."

Max nodded. "I think it's time to split up. You need to make friends with that girl, find out what

you can about the chimney sweep. I'll follow the boy and ask about a job. I need to be there and see if I can catch the chimney sweep red-handed."

Katie was glaring at her brother.

"Er, what's wrong, Katie?" he asked.

"School? You want me to go to school, while you go on an adventure? Are you having a laugh?" she shrieked.

"Shhhh," said Max. "Being a chimney sweep was a boy's job. Besides, school wasn't compulsory for children over the age of ten until 1893. Sorry Sis', but I'm too old for school!"

Katie was not happy, as she watched Max disappear down the street after the boy. She was sure she could see a smile on Max's face as he turned the corner.

7

Katie stepped inside the school gates and approached the girl with the ribbons. She decided to pretend she was a new girl in school.

"Hi, I'm Katie," she said. "I'm new here and don't know where I should go."

"Hello!" replied the girl with a beaming smile. "I'm Cynthia. Do you want to play hopscotch?"

Katie nodded, although she didn't know how to play. She watched Cynthia and the other girls roll a stone and then hop and jump inside the squares while the other girls counted together. When it was Katie's turn, she knew what to do.

Katie was giggling and having a lovely time. She forgot she had to go to school. Soon, the bell rang and the children all lined up. Katie followed Cynthia.

There was a separate entrance for boys and girls.

The sign was carved into the stone above the doors and there was one line of boys and one line of girls in different parts of the playground.

Everyone was silent.

The girls were led in silence and single-file up some creaky wooden stairs to a classroom, where everyone sat down at desks facing the front. The classroom was huge. Katie estimated there must be about fifty children in here!

A large blackboard was at the front of the room. The teacher glared at the children in front of her. She held a cane in her hands and had a stern look on her face.

The teacher walked along the rows of desks, saying the six times table one at a time.

"One times six is six," she said.

The class then repeated altogether: "One times six is six."

The teacher continued. "Two times six is twelve."

The class repeated again. This continued all the way until twelve times twelve.

Next, it was time to practise handwriting. Everyone waited until the teacher gave the instruction, then the children lifted the lids of their desk and pulled out a small slate board. They also picked up a slate pen, closed the desk and laid the items flat on the desk.

Katie had never written using a slate pen on a slate board. She waited until the teacher was looking away, then tried writing her name quietly.

The pencil made a sharp screech on her board and the teacher spun round to face the class.

Katie froze. She locked eyes with the teacher and could feel her hands start to shake.

The teacher was by Katie's desk in an instant. She brought her cane down so hard on the desk that the slate board bounced up and clattered back down with a rattle.

The whole class took a frightened deep breath in at once. Nobody dared move.

8

Meanwhile, Max had run after the chimney sweep boy and introduced himself.

"Hi, I'm Max," he said.

The boy smiled and introduced himself as Tom.

Max fell into step with him.

"I'm looking for a job," said Max. "I don't suppose you need any help?"

Tom grinned. "Yes! I do need help! What perfect timing. We have a big job this afternoon. It's a house with four floors and three fire places on every floor. It's too much for me to do on my own. I'll just need to check with the boss, Mr Graves."

Max couldn't believe his luck!

"Here, let me help you carry that brush," said Max. He held it over his shoulder and marched along the street whistling a happy tune.

They reached the corner, where Max turned left

too quickly. The long brush swung in an arc and Tom had to duck out of the way. They both realised what had happened and giggled.

"Quick reactions!" laughed Max.

"I've done the same thing myself!" replied Tom. "The large brush at the end takes a bit of getting used to!"

Max's thoughts returned to the job. "Do you think your boss will be happy for me to work?"

"I hope so. Mr Graves always tries to rush me," continued Tom. "But he doesn't understand how hard it is to clean in the dark with bleeding knees and soot in your lungs. Two of us would be much quicker."

Max's smile was fading fast. Soot? Blood? Tom did this every day and struggled. How on earth had Max thought he could do this?

He had to catch Mr Graves red-handed quickly, before he got hurt.

9

The teacher grabbed Katie's wrist and dragged her out of her seat and to a chair in the corner of the room.

"Sit!" barked the teacher. Katie quickly sat down on the stool and watched as the teacher picked up a large cone with a capital 'D' on the front and placed it on Katie's head.

Katie could feel her cheeks getting hot as she realised she was wearing the dreaded Dunce's Hat. The whole class was looking at her.

The rest of the afternoon's lessons continued, but Katie could only watch. She was never invited to sit back at her desk. She thought about her own school and realised that her own class teacher, Mrs Allen, was so kind and gentle. She would never humiliate one of the children like this.

Katie was very pleased Max couldn't see her now.

D

10

Max and Tom walked along the street and stopped outside a grand house with lots of chimneys. Mr Graves stumbled and joined them at the steps.

Tom introduced Max and explained that he was looking for a job.

Max shrunk under the stare of Mr Graves.

"First day is unpaid," he grumbled. "I need to see if you can do the job before I give you any money."

Max wanted to argue back, but he had no choice. He had to agree. He nodded his head in answer.

They entered the house through the servants' entrance, which was below the ground level. The grumpy maid told them to leave their grubby shoes there, then showed them to the first room upstairs.

They got busy covering all the furniture with large sheets. Max watched Mr Graves cover the most comfortable-looking chair, then sit down heavily on top of the dust sheet. He wiggled from side to side as he got himself comfortable, then closed his eyes. Max couldn't believe it!

Tom saw Max's expression and shrugged. "He always falls asleep while I do all the work."

"Come on, this flue's short but wide, so you'll be able to see what I'm doing," said Tom.

Max watched Tom climb the vertical chimney flue using his knees, feet and elbows, while cleaning with the brush as he went. Max coughed as a cloud of soot fell down and landed on his up-turned face.

Every now and then, Max glanced over to Mr Graves, who was now snoring loudly. The maid was standing guard at the door, watching. Nothing could possibly be stolen here.

After a while, Tom climbed back down. He was covered in soot and his knees were grazed.

On the way to the fireplace in the next room, Tom nudged Mr Graves, who woke up grumbling.

Tom went up first and said he would do the top half, while Max could stay lower and clean the bottom half.

Max started climbing. He was much slower than Tom, who seemed to climb effortlessly. Max cried out in pain as the rough bricks inside the chimney dug into his skin. He shifted his weight to ease the pain, but found himself slipping.

Max called out for help, but when he looked up, Tom was nowhere in sight. For a split second, he was very impressed with how quickly Tom must climb, but he was quickly reminded of the shooting pain in his knees and elbows.

Just as he was about to call for help again, he heard a strange noise, like a crackling sound. Was this Mr Graves starting to thieve? He listened carefully, trying not to move, when he smelt something. He recognised the smell but what was it? He coughed and realised what the smell was.

No… Surely not...

It smelt like smoke.

He looked down and yelled out in fear. There were flames in the fireplace below! Mr Graves had lit a fire to flush him out. The flames were starting to grow higher. He could feel the heat on his bare feet and his lungs were straining from the smoke that was swirling around him. He could feel panic start to rise in his chest. He was trapped.

And alone.

11

Katie always looked forward to the bell at home time, but she had never felt so happy and relieved as she did now.

The teacher dismissed the children one by one, until Katie was the only child left in the classroom.

"You in the corner are dismissed," she said eventually, without even looking in Katie's direction.

Katie left the hat on the stool and tried to speak. No words would come out! Her throat was dry and she wanted to leave as quickly as she could. She gave an awkward bow of the head and mumbled 'thank you', then tiptoed towards the door.

She had to find Cynthia.

Katie rushed down the creaking stairs and outside into the empty playground.

Katie's shoulders slumped and she kicked a pebble on the ground. Cynthia was gone.

Katie felt guilty. If she had just followed the rules, she would have left at the same time as Cynthia and had a chance to talk to her.

Katie left through the school gates and leaned against a wall feeling helpless.

"You were very lucky in there!" laughed a voice beside Katie.

It was Cynthia! She had waited! Katie grinned from ear to ear.

"Lucky?!" exclaimed Katie. "That was the most embarrassing and the most boring experience of my entire life!"

Cynthia frowned. "But it could have been a lot worse. You could have been caned. Now THAT is embarrassing," shivered Cynthia. "AND painful."

Katie's eyes widened at the thought of being hit with a stick by a teacher. "Really? She can do that? To children?"

Cynthia laughed. "Of course! I've been caned

many times. Why do you think I follow the rules so well?!"

Katie decided it was now or never.

"I guess it's time to go home now. Where do you live?" she asked.

Cynthia looked a bit uncomfortable and hesitated before she answered. "Er, just a little place not far from here. It's just me and my brother," she explained sadly. "We're orphans."

Katie was shocked. "What, you have no adults to look after you?"

Katie thought how lucky Cynthia was. No adults meant no rules. Just fun! You could make up your own rules! Katie imagined what her house would be like without adults. Ice cream for breakfast, chocolate for lunch and pizza for dinner every day. Instead of school, she'd go to the park all day.

Cynthia shook her head. "No. We look after ourselves. Well, my brother looks after us. He works hard as a chimney sweep to earn money to buy food. He makes sure I have clothes so I can go to school. I feel guilty every day, but he says it's important for one of us to get an education. He wants me to escape this life, to make something of myself."

Katie suddenly felt horribly guilty about wishing she didn't have to go to school. She was lucky that she could get an education.

"What's it like where you live?" asked Katie.

Cynthia shrugged. "We sleep where we can. We huddle together to keep warm. There are a lot of people who live there. A lot of shouting and arguments between the adults. People take stuff too. We have to sleep wearing our clothes. Once, I woke up and my shoes were gone."

Katie felt especially guilty now. Her adults looked after her. They kept her safe.

12

Max was clinging on for dear life as the flames started to fly up towards him, licking his toes.

Just as he was starting to slip, he heard Tom call his name from above.

"Max, listen to me," he called. "Keep your head

up! Look this way! You have to climb or you will suffocate!"

Max lifted his head to look at Tom. He couldn't see him through the smoke, but he wasn't alone any more.

"I know it hurts, but you have to climb," urged Tom. "Use the edges of your feet, push your whole body against the sides, do what you have to do, just CLIMB!"

Max knew he was right. He used all his strength and pushed upwards. He didn't move much, but it was a start. He forced himself to ignore the sharp pain on his knees and pushed higher.

"That's it!" cried Tom. "You're nearly at the top!"

Max followed Tom's voice and started to feel cool air above. Max felt Tom's hands grip his wrists and help pull him to safety on the rooftop.

Max fell onto the tiles and gulped in clean breaths of the night air.

"That's what they do when a boy gets stuck," said Tom sadly. "They light a fire to hurry them up."

Max was horrified. "I could have died! Doesn't he care?!"

Tom shrugged. "We're just orphans," explained Tom. "Nobody cares about us. We have to stick together and survive."

It was the saddest thing Max had ever heard.

13

Max and Tom were sitting on the roof looking out across the rooftops of the city. Thick plumes of smoke were belching out of the tall, thin chimneys of the nearby factory. Birds darted in between the chimney stacks.

Max had never imagined what it must look like up here. You could walk from one end of the road to the other across the rooftops of these terraced houses. It felt like another world, a world free from adults.

"How long have you been a chimney sweep?" asked Max.

"Six years," replied Tom.

Max was shocked. "But you were so young! Have you never been to school?"

Tom shook his head. "Until the Ragged Schools opened, school was only for rich kids."

“What’s a Ragged School?” asked Max.

“It’s a free school that is paid for by a rich business man,” explained Tom. “My sister goes to one just down the road. She’s really clever. She can read and write!”

“Why don’t you go too, if it’s free?” asked Max.

“We still need to eat,” replied Tom. “I work so we can survive.”

Max realised it was a hard life for Tom and his sister. He knew their story wasn’t unusual, that lots of people in Victorian times struggled to survive.

“Right, we should go,” said Tom. “We don’t want Mr Graves to get angry with us.”

Max noticed something fall from Tom’s pocket as he stood up. He reached out to pick it up to give it back when he stopped.

It was a beautiful necklace with dark green beads. The two boys froze. They looked at each other.

“Is this what I think it is?” asked Max.

14

Tom lowered his eyes in shame, but soon his expression changed to anger.

"I work until my skin is grazed and bruised every day and all I earn is a few pennies a week!" explained Tom. "It's not enough to pay for both of us to eat, let alone stay somewhere safe and warm and clean."

"I understand it's hard," reasoned Max, "but what about the people you're stealing from?"

"They're rich, they can afford it! They'll never have to walk barefoot or sleep on the street," argued Tom. "They have so many jewels they don't know what to do with them! Most don't even notice they're missing."

"Not today," said Max. "Mr and Mrs Green decided it must be the servant who was watching over you. That servant girl lost her job today. She doesn't know how she's going to survive herself now."

Tom's eyes widened.

"I didn't realise!" he sobbed. "I… I… I just thought they wouldn't even notice."

Max put his arm round Tom's shoulders to comfort him.

"It's OK," soothed Max. "But I think you know

what you have to do now."

Tom's head snapped up. "I can't give it back! They'll call the police and arrest me and I'll go to prison or the workhouse or the orphanage and never see Cynthia again! She'll have to get a job and never get a good education and this will all have been for nothing."

15

"I need to meet my brother now," said Cynthia. "He should be finishing work soon."

Katie grinned. "Me too! I'm meeting my brother round the corner. Maybe we can walk together?"

They walked round the corner and chatted until they reached the house.

Max and Tom were already there, waiting.

They didn't look happy.

"Is everything OK?" asked Cynthia when they got closer.

Tom wouldn't meet her eyes. "I'm sorry, Cynthia. I have something to confess."

16

The four children were standing at the bottom step of Mr and Mrs Green's house. The large door towered high above them.

Cynthia had been very understanding, but she agreed they needed to do the right thing and return the jewellery.

Tom was frowning and chewing his fingernails anxiously. He kept looking around, as if searching for an escape route.

Max was desperately trying to think of some wise words to convince Tom that this was the right thing to do, when Tom surprised them all. He held his hands firmly by his sides, marched up the stairs and knocked on the door with the round brass knocker. The others climbed the steps to join him.

They didn't have to wait long before the door was answered by a servant. She took one look at the bare-footed boys covered in soot and started to close the door. "No thank you, no sweeping needed."

Just as the door was about to close, Katie pushed her foot just inside to stop it from closing.

"Please listen to us. We are here about the jewellery that was taken," she said. "We would like to speak to Mr and Mrs Green."

At that moment, the lady of the house was walking through the hallway and overheard Katie.

"It's OK, Eliza," she said. "Let them in. I'd like to hear what they have to say."

They were led inside to the drawing room, much to Eliza's disgust, where Mr Green joined them.

Katie's eyes were wide as she admired the room. It had high ceilings with a beautiful crystal chandelier hanging down. The large fireplace had colourful tiles with a pretty pattern.

Tom took a deep breath and put his hand in his pocket. He pulled out the jewellery that he had taken earlier this morning.

Mrs Green gasped and reached out for her beloved necklace, smiling at him. "However did you find this?"

"Find it? I… er..." Tom was struggling to find the right words. But again, just when the others were about to step in to help him, Tom stood up straight, looked at Mr and Mrs Green, and spoke clearly. "I didn't find it, I took it. I stole from you and I am very, very, very sorry. I am ashamed of what I have done and hope you can forgive me."

Mrs Green was shocked. "But, why? Why would you steal from us?"

"Me and my sister Cynthia are orphans. I work hard sweeping chimneys to earn a few pence every week, but it is never enough to feed us both and pay for somewhere safe to sleep. I want her to go to school, so at least one of us can get out of the slums. But no excuses, I know that what I did was wrong and I am here to say sorry. I will understand if you call the police."

Mrs Green wiped tears from her eyes.

"But how? How on earth did you get inside the locked room?" she asked.

Everyone looked at Tom. Nobody else had thought to ask him this!

"I climbed up the chimney and down through the next one into the locked room," explained Tom.

At that moment, there was another knock at the door. Max looked at the large grandfather clock in the corner. It was six o'clock. It must be Peggy.

Everyone listened as Eliza walked to the door. Max's eyes were following the long pendulum of the clock as it swung left... right... left...

The clock chimed six times.

Just as the clock quietened, Eliza returned with Peggy.

Mr and Mrs Green turned to her and apologised

for not believing that she was innocent. "I'm so very sorry, Peggy," said Mr Green. "We would like you to stay, if you'll forgive us?"

Peggy beamed at them. "Thank you, I would love to come back!"

Mrs Green turned to Tom. "I am very impressed that you came here to face up to your mistake," she said. "I know it wasn't easy to come here. I respect that. But more importantly, I am sorry that your life has been so hard. You are children. You should both be in school, enjoying your childhood and most importantly you should feel safe."

Mrs Green looked at her husband, who nodded. "We would like you to come and live here with us. We have this big house, this big empty house, and I think what it's missing is children."

Tom's head lifted in shock. "You... you… you want us to live here? With you?"

Mrs Green nodded.

Tom frowned. "Is this a trick so you can keep us here while we wait for the police to turn up?"

"No!" laughed Mr Green. "You will be happy here, I promise."

Tom and Cynthia looked at each other with wide eyes. They couldn't believe their luck!

It felt like a good moment to leave. Max and Katie wished everyone well and quietly stepped out into the street. It was time for the Time Machine to work its magic. If it still could.

17

The wind picked up speed. Leaves swirled and a rainbow of colours wrapped around Max and Katie like a blanket. They were going back to modern day.

As soon as they were safely back in their own home in the 21st century, they got changed back into their jeans and t-shirts. Max went to the bathroom to wash the soot off his face.

Katie was busy looking out of the window at the chimneys of the Victorian houses in their street and beyond, imagining how many children had scrambled onto these rooftops in the past.

When Max returned with a face clean of soot, they heard Mum calling them back downstairs to finish their homework.

“Come on,” said Katie. “Let’s get our homework finished.”

Max was shocked into silence. Katie wasn’t

making crazy excuses. She wasn't trying to hide or pretend to be asleep.

Katie actually wanted to get her homework done.

"Wha... what... are you OK?" he spluttered.

Katie took a deep breath. "We're so lucky that we can go to school and feel safe, that no teacher will ever hit us or embarrass us by putting a stupid hat on us. And we're lucky that we have the freedom to go to school. As annoying as it is, it's a lot better than having to work up chimneys where you could get hurt. We get to have an education, unlike many children in lots of countries across the world still today."

Max was shocked into silence once again. He nodded, grinned and followed his sister down the stairs to finish their homework. He was impressed.

But he also knew she would be moaning within fifteen minutes of picking up her homework book.

He was wrong. It only took five.

See you on our next adventure!

Also in the Mysteries in Time series:

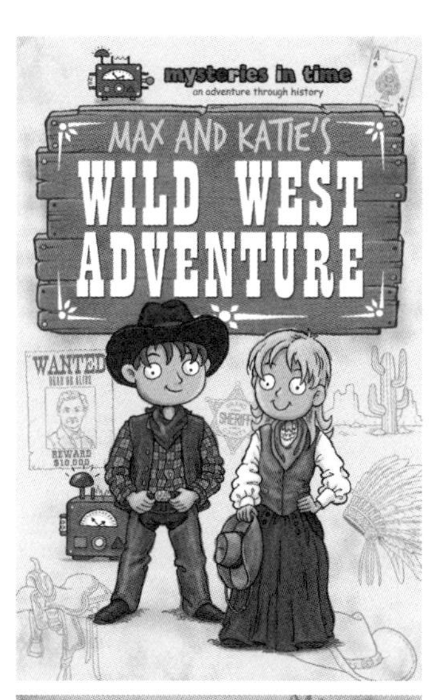
mysteries in time
an adventure through history
MAX AND KATIE'S
WILD WEST
ADVENTURE
WANTED
SHERIFF
REWARD
$10,000

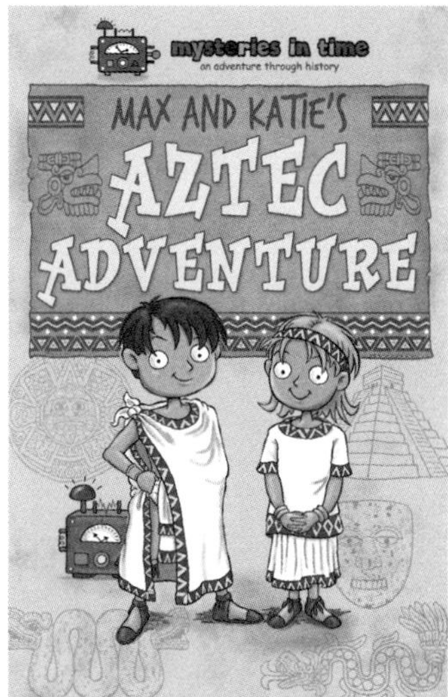
mysteries in time
an adventure through history
MAX AND KATIE'S
AZTEC
ADVENTURE

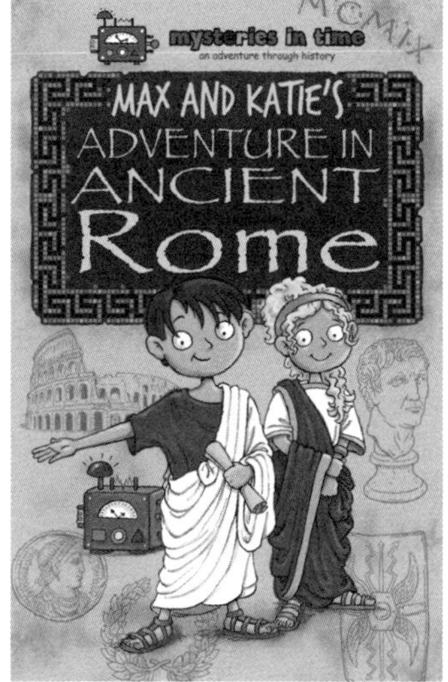
mysteries in time
an adventure through history
MCMIX
MAX AND KATIE'S
ADVENTURE IN
ANCIENT
Rome

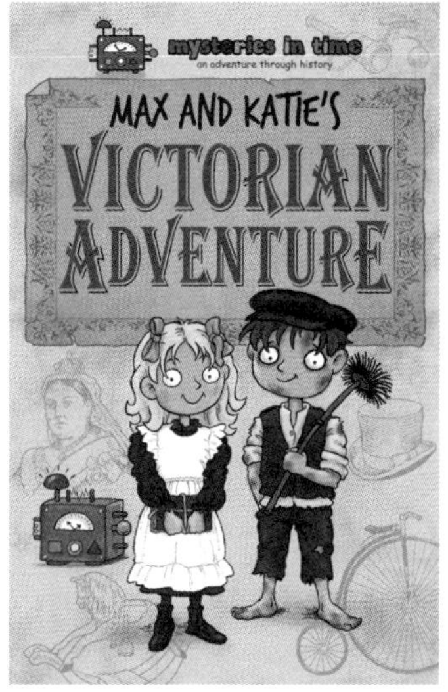
mysteries in time
an adventure through history
MAX AND KATIE'S
VICTORIAN
ADVENTURE

mysteries in time
an adventure through history
MAX AND KATIE'S
VIKING
ADVENTURE

新年快乐
mysteries in time
an adventure through history
MAX AND KATIE'S
ADVENTURE
IN ANCIENT
CHINA

mysteries in time
an adventure through history
MAX AND KATIE'S
SPACE
ADVENTURE

mysteries in time
an adventure through history
MAX AND KATIE'S
STUART
ADVENTURE